Stanley's Little Sister

Written by
Linda Bailey

Illustrated by
Bill Slavin

KIDS CAN PRESS

Stanley knew he wasn't supposed to chase the cat.

But this was Stanley's house! It wasn't supposed to *have* a cat. And who invited that cat to live here anyway?

Stanley's people, that's who. They came home with the cat, and that was that.

"Nobody asked *me*," thought Stanley.

But he knew he was supposed to be a good dog. So he trotted over, and he gave that cat a great big, friendly sniff.

THWACK! went the cat's paw, right across his nose.

"ROWP!" yelped Stanley. "Hey! No fair!"

He turned to his people. He let out a pitiful whine. They weren't even looking his way!

Well, *somebody* had to explain things to the cat.

"KARFF! KARFF! KARFF! KARFF!" explained Stanley.

And there, right in front of his nose, the cat puffed up. She rose to her toes and swelled into a huge hissy hairball. Then she ...

Ran!

Stanley *knew* he wasn't supposed to chase her. He *tried* to stop himself. But he just couldn't help it!

"CREEEOWRRRR!" screeched the cat.

Stanley couldn't believe how fast she could climb a curtain.

"STANLEY!" yelled his people. "LEAVE THE CAT ALONE!"

"Awwrrr," thought Stanley as they dragged him into the bathroom and shut the door. "I was just trying to make friends."

Luckily, he had some *real* friends in the dog park — Alice and Nutsy and Gassy Jack.

"I tried to be nice," Stanley told them. "*She* started it!"

"I know what you mean," said Gassy Jack. "My people blame me for everything."

"We got a new hamster once," said Alice. "It was rrrrrufff!"

Little Nutsy had an idea. "You're awfully big," she told Stanley. "Maybe if you weren't so big ..."

So Stanley decided to be smaller. He lay flat on his belly and creepy-crawled up to the cat.

"Hi there!" said Stanley, with his nose in the carpet.

"Hsssst!" said the cat.

"She doesn't understand dog talk," thought Stanley. His people didn't understand, either. It led to all kinds of problems.

"A lick is nice," thought Stanley. "Everyone likes a lick." He sat up and gave her a big, wet one.

"SCREEEEEEE!" howled the cat as she shot down the hall.

Stanley *tried* not to chase her. But something came over him ...

This time, he ended up in the laundry room.

The next day, Stanley was surprised to see a new dish of food on the floor.

"Yum!" thought Stanley. "I don't mind if I do."

"Hsssst!" said the cat.

"Stanley!" said his people. "Leave Fluffy's food ALONE!"

"Well, garsh," thought Stanley as they hauled him into the furnace room. "Nobody told *me* it was Fluffy's food."

And then there was the problem of the couch. When his people sat on the couch, the cat sat on their laps. Stanley wondered why *he* never got to sit on his people's laps. He decided to give it a try.

"Oh, for heaven's sake, Stanley," said his people. "Get OFF!"

Stanley had to go back on the floor. He was lying there when the cat scampered down.

"I *won't* chase her," Stanley said to himself. "I won't, I won't, I won't. This time, for sure."

But he did.

He chased her.

That night he slept on the porch.

"She hates me," said Stanley to his friends.

"She doesn't *hate* you," said Alice. "She just doesn't know you."

"Maybe she could be your little sister," said Nutsy.

"I don't *want* a little sister!" said Stanley.

"Maybe you should stop chasing her," said Gassy Jack.

The dogs all let out huge sighs. They knew how hard *that* would be.

Stanley decided to give it one last try. He gathered up his favorite toys.

"Hey, you!" he said, pushing his nose under the couch, where the cat was hiding. "Want to play with Chewy Rabbit? Or look! Here's Squeaky Bear!"

Of course, he said it in dog talk. And of course, she didn't understand.

Neither did his people. "STANLEY!" they yelled. "LEAVE THE CAT ALONE!"

Stanley flopped down on the carpet. "That's it!" he sniffed. "I can't do anything right. I give up."

He lay there, perfectly still, for a very long time — so long, he almost fell asleep. When he heard rustling under the couch, he didn't move. When he heard the cat padding around him, he *still* didn't move. He didn't even move when she rubbed up against him.

And then an amazing thing happened. The cat lay down. Right beside Stanley. Fur to fur! She closed her eyes and made a soft cat-sound. It was almost like a growl ... but different.

"Purrrrr," said the cat.

Stanley didn't know cat talk, but he thought he understood.

"She likes me!" thought Stanley. "She really LIKES me!"

He stayed still and quiet, except for one little sound.

"Purrrrrrrrrrrr," said Stanley.

After a while, he heard his people come in. When they saw Stanley and his little sister lying there together, they made a soft people-sound.

"Awwwww," they said. Then they quietly tiptoed away.

Stanley fell asleep.

And so did the cat.

And that was that.

To my own little sisters, Debbie and Wendy, with love — L.B.

To Merlin, prince among cats — B.S.

Text © 2010 Linda Bailey
Illustrations © 2010 Bill Slavin

Kids Can Press acknowledges the financial support of the Government of Ontario,
through the Ontario Media Development Corporation's Ontario Book Initiative;
the Ontario Arts Council; the Canada Council for the Arts; and the Government
of Canada, through the BPIDP, for our publishing activity.

Published in Canada by
Kids Can Press Ltd.
29 Birch Avenue
Toronto, ON M4V 1E2

Published in the U.S. by
Kids Can Press Ltd.
2250 Military Road
Tonawanda, NY 14150

www.kidscanpress.com

The artwork in this book was rendered in acrylics, on gessoed paper.
The text is set in Leawood Medium.

Edited by Tara Walker
Designed by Julia Naimska

This book is smyth sewn casebound.
Manufactured in Tseung Kwan O, Kowloon Hong Kong, China,
in 4/2010 by Paramount Printing Co. Ltd.

CM 10 0 9 8 7 6 5 4 3 2 1

Library and Archives Canada Cataloguing in Publication

Bailey, Linda, 1948–
Stanley's little sister / written by Linda Bailey ; illustrated by Bill Slavin.

ISBN 978-1-55453-487-6 (bound)

I. Slavin, Bill II. Title.

PS8553.A3644S733 2010   jC813'.54   C2009-906865-6

Kids Can Press is a *l'orus*™ Entertainment company